Hurry Up, Christmas!

Hurry Up, Christmas!

By Clay Graves

Drawings by Fred M. Irvin

GARRARD PUBLISHING COMPANY

CHAMPAIGN, ILLINOIS

Copyright © 1976 by Clay Graves   All rights reserved. Manufactured in the U.S.A.
International Standard Book Number: 0–8116–6068–0   Library of Congress Catalog Card Number: 75-11504

Hurry Up, Christmas!

"When will it be Christmas?"
asked Susie.
"Soon," said her father.

"Will Christmas come soon?"
asked Susie.

"Soon," said her mother.

"I wish Christmas would hurry," said Susie.

"Will Christmas come soon?"
asked Susie.

"It won't be long,"
said grandfather.

"I wish Christmas would hurry,"
said Susie.

"There are just
ten more days,"
said grandmother.

13

"Will Christmas come soon?"
asked Susie.

"Soon,"
said her teacher.

"I wish Christmas would hurry,"
said Susie.

"Just a few more days,"
said father.

"I can't wait for Christmas!"
said Susie.

"Just four more days,"
said her brother.

"The tree is ready
for Christmas
and so am I,"
said Susie.

"I have a present for you,"
said Susie.

"Hurry up, Christmas!"
said Susie.

"Christmas is tomorrow,"
Susie said happily.

"Merry Christmas, everybody!"
shouted Susie.

"Christmas hurried up,"
Susie said.
"Now I wish it
would slow down!"